*To my beloved son Andrei*

Published in 2003 by Simply Read Books Inc.

Cataloguing in Publication Data

James, Elizabeth, 1958-
The little black hen / Antony Pogorelsky, author;
retold by Elizabeth James; Gennady Spirin, illustrator

Translation of: Cherna_i_a kuri_t_sa, ili, Podzemnye zhiteli.
ISBN 1-894965-03-5

I. Chickens--Folklore. 2. Folklore--Russia. I. Spirin, Gennadii. II.
Pogorelski_i, Antoni_i, 1787-1836. Cherna_i_a kuri_t_sa, ili, Podzemnye
zhiteli. English. III. Title.
PS8569.A4335L57 2003     j398.2'0947     C2003-910259-9
PZ8.J35Li 2003

Copyright © 2002 Esslinger Verlag

Printed and bound in Belgium

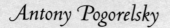

Antony Pogorelsky

# THE LITTLE BLACK HEN

*Illustrated by Gennady Spirin*

*Retold by*
*Elizabeth James*

Simply Read Books

There once was a boy named Alyosha who was sent to the best boarding school in the beautiful city of St. Petersburg. He enjoyed his life at school and had many friends.

Alyosha never went home to his parents in the country because it was too far away. During school holidays and Sundays, when his friends were away with their families, he sometimes felt bored and lonely.

When Alyosha was alone, he spent the long winter evenings reading books about the heroic knights of days long ago. He knew by heart the stories about their battles and brave deeds, the great kings and queens, and their magnificent castles.

In the afternoons, Alyosha played with the chickens in the courtyard. His special favourite was a little black hen he called Blackey. The little black hen loved Alyosha and let him stroke his feathers.

One day the cook appeared in the courtyard with a big knife and called to Alyosha, "Help me catch the little black hen!"

She caught his wing and raised her knife. Alyosha thought he heard the voice of his beloved hen crying, "Save me, save me. I'm frightened, Alyosha!"

Alyosha ran to the cook and pushed her away from Blackey with all his strength. "Please don't kill my little black hen!" pleaded Alyosha. "If you spare his life, I'll give you a gold coin."

He gave her a gold coin that his grandmother had given him. The cook put the gold coin in her pocket when she was sure that no one was watching, and Blackey was saved.

Later that night, Alyosha couldn't fall asleep. He lay in bed and listened as the familiar noises in the dormitory drifted away slowly. Everything was quiet at last, until he heard a small voice calling his name.

The little black hen appeared from under the next bed and whispered, "Don't be afraid, Alyosha. Get dressed quickly and follow me."

Alyosha laughed, "How can I get dressed in the dark?"

Blackey flapped his wings and suddenly the room filled with the sparkle of silvery lights, no bigger than Alyosha's thumb. He jumped out of bed and put on his clothes.

"Keep silent and don't touch anything!" said Blackey.

Bravely, Alyosha did as he was told and followed the little black hen a long way through a series of dark and winding corridors to a set of hidden rooms.

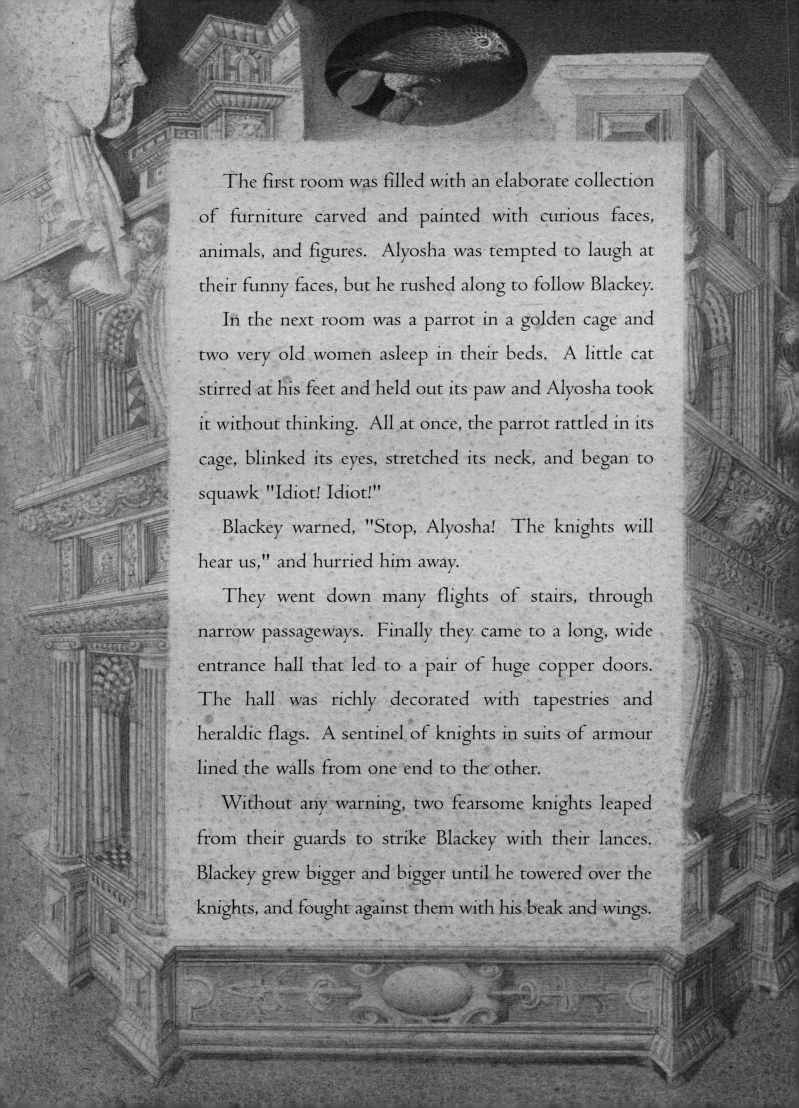

The first room was filled with an elaborate collection of furniture carved and painted with curious faces, animals, and figures. Alyosha was tempted to laugh at their funny faces, but he rushed along to follow Blackey.

In the next room was a parrot in a golden cage and two very old women asleep in their beds. A little cat stirred at his feet and held out its paw and Alyosha took it without thinking. All at once, the parrot rattled in its cage, blinked its eyes, stretched its neck, and began to squawk "Idiot! Idiot!"

Blackey warned, "Stop, Alyosha! The knights will hear us," and hurried him away.

They went down many flights of stairs, through narrow passageways. Finally they came to a long, wide entrance hall that led to a pair of huge copper doors. The hall was richly decorated with tapestries and heraldic flags. A sentinel of knights in suits of armour lined the walls from one end to the other.

Without any warning, two fearsome knights leaped from their guards to strike Blackey with their lances. Blackey grew bigger and bigger until he towered over the knights, and fought against them with his beak and wings.

Alyosha watched in terror as the room began to revolve, and he collapsed in a faint. When he opened his eyes, he was lying in his own bed the next morning. He longed to find out if Blackey was safe, but a snowstorm kept him inside all day.

That night, the little black hen returned to Alyosha and said, "Luckily, I escaped the knights. You must listen carefully to me this time. Promise me you'll be quiet and won't touch anything!"

Alyosha dressed and followed Blackey from room to room, doing exactly as he was told. He paid no attention to the funny faces, crept past the old women sleeping, the parrot blinking, and the cat licking its paws.

When they entered the big hall, the knights stood silently on guard. The little black hen flapped his wings and their armour shattered and they fell apart in a hundred pieces.

The huge copper doors opened and Alyosha entered a golden, miniature throne room. A large procession of little people, arrayed in regal clothes, came to receive Alyosha and presented him ceremoniously to the king. Alyosha bowed deeply, and waited for the king to speak.

"We are grateful to you. You have done a great service to my people," said the king, "And you deserve a reward for saving the life of my faithful ambassador." The king introduced a round little man dressed in black, wearing a white lace collar and a red feathered hat. Alyosha instantly recognized Blackey when the ambassador stepped closely and smiled at him.

"What do you wish me to grant you?" asked the king.

"Speak bravely," whispered the ambassador to Alyosha.

Alyosha needed more time to think of a better answer but all he could do was blurt out, "I wish I knew all the answers at school and never had to study."

The king frowned, "I didn't know you were such a lazy boy, Alyosha, but I promised to grant you a wish and so be it!" He waved his hand, and a servant brought him a tiny seed of corn on a gold tray. The king gave the seed to Alyosha, and said "Keep it with you always and you'll know all your lessons at school. You will stay in my favour only if you obey my command and keep this a secret. If you tell anyone about our underground kingdom, you will destroy our happiness and bring us great hardship."

Alyosha gave his word to the king, and carefully put the tiny seed in his pocket. The king ordered a great feast and Alyosha fell asleep after the celebrations.

The next morning he woke in his own bed and wondered if the underground kingdom was just a dream. He felt inside his pocket and gasped in amazement, because the magic seed was still there.

The school holidays finally ended, and Alyosha could hardly wait to know if the magic seed would work. Just as the king promised, the wish came true and Alyosha began to astonish his teachers and school friends with his amazing abilities. His answers were always right and he knew all his lessons without having to study.

The teachers praised him constantly, but a voice inside Alyosha told him it wasn't deserved because it was only due to magic. As time went by, he gradually ignored his feelings and acted as though he was smarter and better than anyone else was at school. Soon his friends and the other students began to resent him.

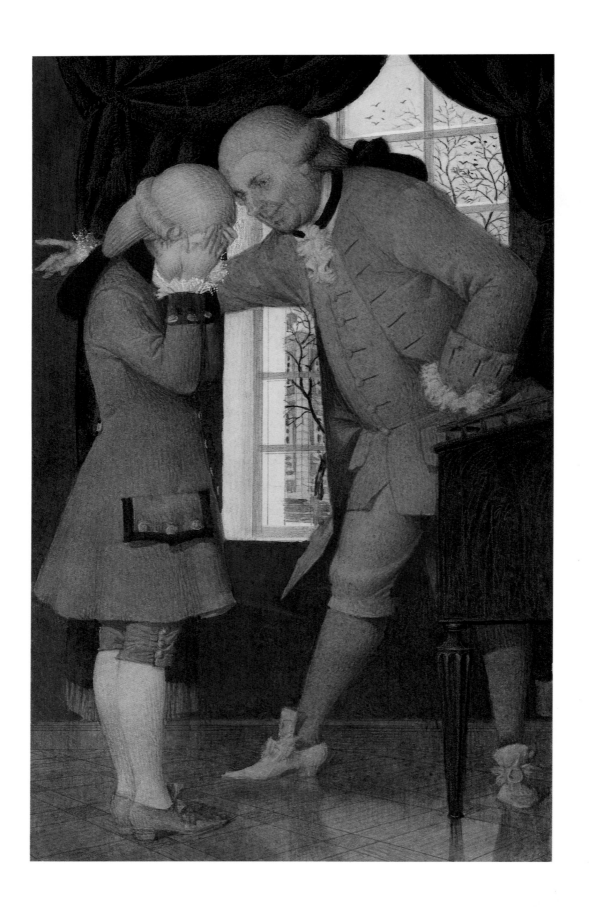

Eventually the teacher decided to reprimand Alyosha's insolence and gave him an impossible task to memorize twenty pages for the next class. Alyosha shrugged his shoulders without a care and went to play, without doubting that he would pass the test with the help of the magic seed.

The next day, Alyosha stood ready in front of the classroom. He cleared his throat to begin, but his face turned many colours and he couldn't say a single word. The entire class laughed and ridiculed him. Speechless, he reached into his pocket, but the seed wasn't there! Alyosha felt helpless and began to cry.

"I've lost my patience with you, Alyosha," said the teacher. "Go to your room and stay there until you have memorized everything!"

Alyosha searched everywhere in his room for the magic seed, but couldn't find it. Over and over, he cried, "Blackey, come and help me, my little black hen! You're my only friend. Have you forgotten me?" Alyosha kept sobbing, but Blackey never appeared and, finally, he cried himself to sleep.

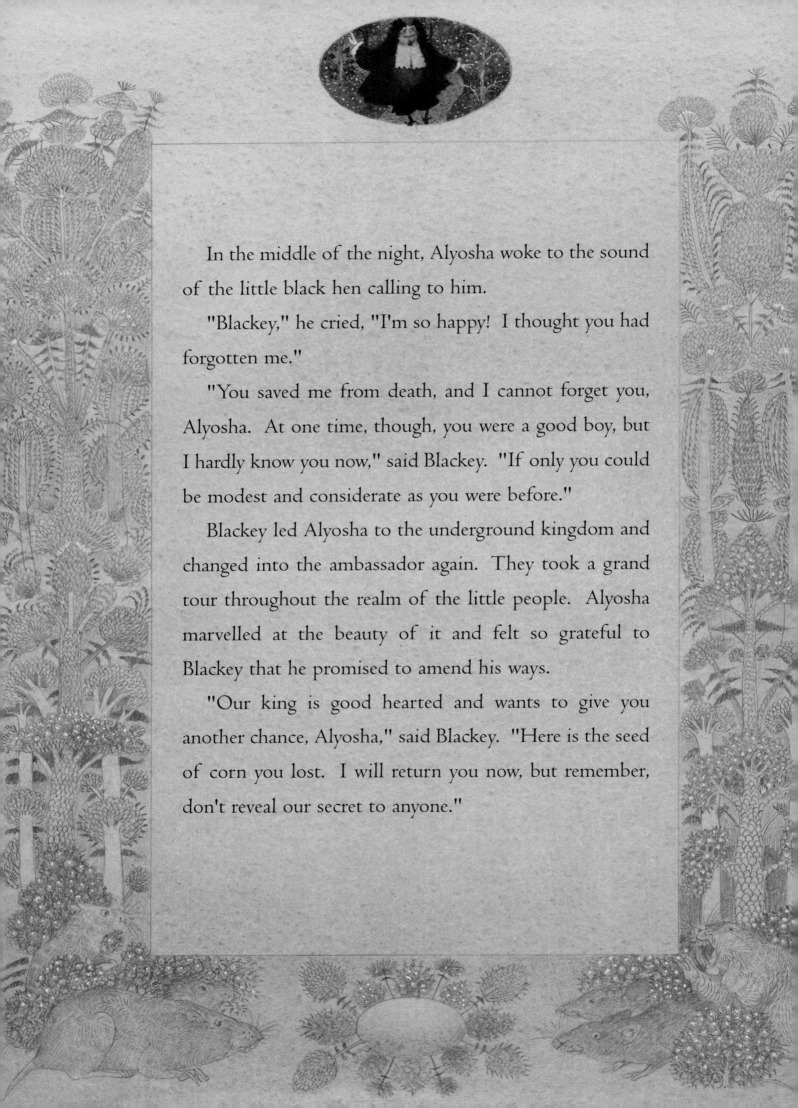

In the middle of the night, Alyosha woke to the sound of the little black hen calling to him.

"Blackey," he cried, "I'm so happy! I thought you had forgotten me."

"You saved me from death, and I cannot forget you, Alyosha. At one time, though, you were a good boy, but I hardly know you now," said Blackey. "If only you could be modest and considerate as you were before."

Blackey led Alyosha to the underground kingdom and changed into the ambassador again. They took a grand tour throughout the realm of the little people. Alyosha marvelled at the beauty of it and felt so grateful to Blackey that he promised to amend his ways.

"Our king is good hearted and wants to give you another chance, Alyosha," said Blackey. "Here is the seed of corn you lost. I will return you now, but remember, don't reveal our secret to anyone."

In the morning, Alyosha went to class with the seed of corn stored safely in his pocket.

His teacher asked sternly, "Do you know your lesson?"

Without a stutter or pause, Alyosha repeated every page to the amazement of his teacher and classmates.

"This is a trick! Alyosha must have cheated! He never had a book in his hands," the class exclaimed.

"When did you study?" asked the teacher.

Alyosha was so speechless and agitated that he couldn't answer. The teacher threatened to punish him and called for the strap. Alyosha suddenly lost his senses and confessed everything. He told them the story about the little black hen and the magical underground kingdom of the little people until he realized his terrible mistake, and began to cry. Tearfully, he reached into his pocket for the seed of corn but it was gone forever.

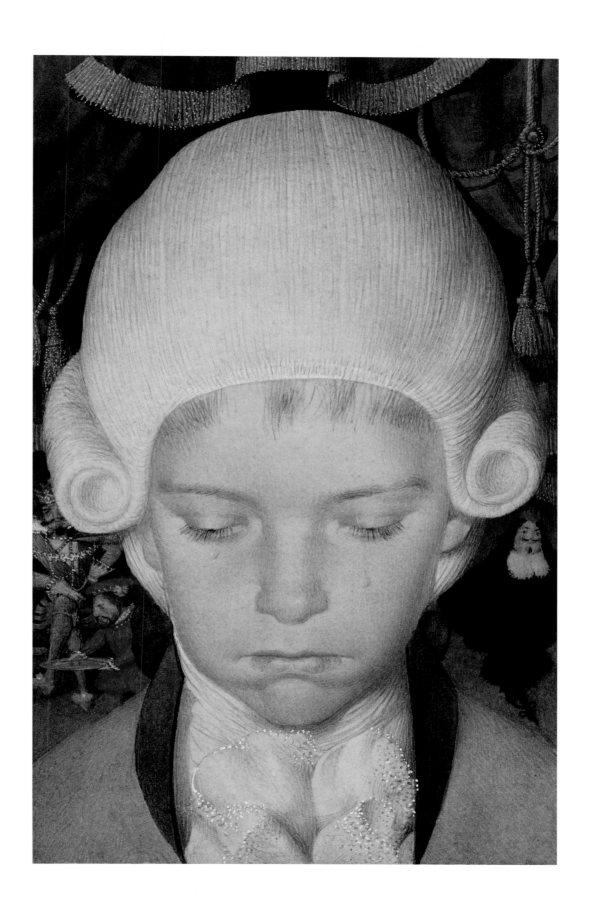

The little black hen disappeared from the courtyard that day. Alyosha waited until after dark, crying in anguish, hoping that Blackey would return and forgive him for breaking his promise. When midnight came, Blackey appeared and spoke to him softly, "Stop crying, Alyosha. I've come one last time to say goodbye."

"Please forgive me, if you can. I'm sorry for breaking my promise," wept Alyosha.

"You saved my life and I will always love you, but in a very short time, I must go." said the ambassador. "Our law states that, if our secret is revealed, we must leave the underground kingdom and move to far away lands. We have lived here in peace and happiness for centuries but now we are heartbroken."

Alyosha reached tenderly for Blackey's tiny hands and was horrified to see that he was handcuffed in gold shackles. Blackey sighed, "This is my punishment for your mistake. Don't cry for me. Your tears cannot help me. I'll be comforted only if you'll become a kind and worthy boy again. Good-bye, Alyosha!" he said, and disappeared.

The following day, Alyosha heard rumblings beneath his feet. He laid down flat, put his ear to the floorboards, and listened to the sound of wheels grinding and the tragic voices of the little people marching away from their underground homes. Above the cries of many tragic voices, he heard Blackey's voice calling out "So long, Alyosha, so long!"

Alyosha didn't move and was later found unconscious, sick with fever. His illness lasted six weeks and the doctors feared for his recovery. The teachers and schoolchildren took pity on him, and never mentioned the past again. Finally he got better and returned to classes, determined to set a fine example and, from that day forward, he studied and worked hard at school.

No one asked him to memorize twenty pages again, but then he couldn't have done it even if he tried.

*The End*